HEATHCLIFF®
GOES TO HOLLYWOOD

Illustrated by Nancy Beiman
Written by Suzanne Weyn

Watermill Press

Published by Watermill Press under License by Marvel Books, a New World Company
ISBN 0-8167-1263-8

It's a beautiful new morning—and Heathcliff is ready for breakfast. He helps himself to a bowl of Little Whiskers Cat Crunchies. Mmmmmmmm! Delicious.

Heathcliff reads an ad on the back of the Little Whiskers box. The cat food company is holding a big contest. The winner will win a trip to Hollywood. And that's not all. The winning cat will star in the next Little Whiskers cat food commercial on TV.

This is my big chance, thinks Heathcliff. *I'm going to be a TV star!* All Heathcliff has to do is send in more Little Whiskers boxtops than anyone else. Heathcliff doesn't waste a minute! He starts ripping off boxtops.

CAT CRUNCHIES
LITTLE WHISKERS CAT CRUNCHIES
LITTLE WHISKERS CAT CRUNCHIES
TRIP TO HOLLYWOOD

Heathcliff pulls the boxtops off of all the boxes of Little Whiskers cat food that Grandma Nutmeg has stored in the pantry closet. Five boxtops. That's not enough.

Heathcliff goes to visit his girlfriend Sonja. She gives Heathcliff five more boxtops. Her five plus Heathcliff's five makes ten boxtops. That's still not enough to win the contest.

Heathcliff and Sonja think very hard. Where can they get more boxtops? Suddenly Heathcliff has an idea!

All those garbage cans must be full of old boxes of Little Whiskers cat food! Heathcliff dives right in! What a mess! He throws the garbage all over the place. *This is great!* thinks Heathcliff. He finds all the Little Whiskers boxtops he needs!

LITTLE WHISKERS CAT CRUNCHES

Heathcliff mails his boxtops in to the Little Whiskers Company. Then he waits for a letter telling him whether or not he is the winner.

Heathcliff waits...and waits...and waits. Every day he checks the mailbox to see if he has won. Every day the mailman says the same thing to him: "Sorry Heathcliff. No mail for you today." But one day the mailman says something different. He says: "Here's a letter for you, Heathcliff."

Heathcliff tears open the letter with his sharp cat claws. Rip. Rip. Rip. He's *so* excited! Heathcliff reads the letter. He lets out a meow of joy! He won! He won the contest. He sings a happy song.

"Be quiet!" yell his neighbors. But Heathcliff is too happy to care. They don't know that Heathcliff is going to Hollywood to be a star!

WINNER
1ST PLACE

Now all Heathcliff has to do is tell the Nutmegs that they are all going to Hollywood. He waits for the perfect moment. He wants to make sure they will go.

"I just can't decide where we should go on vacation this year," sighs Grandma Nutmeg.

"I want someplace with beaches," says Iggy.

"I want to go somewhere where there are lots of things to see," adds Grandpa.

"Why, look at Heathcliff," says Grandma. "He looks like he's all set for a trip to Hollywood."

"Say! That's a great idea!" says Grandpa. "Let's go to Hollywood."

Heathcliff whips out his letter from the cat food company and shows Grandpa Nutmeg.

"Well what do you know," Grandpa says. "Let's all get packed. It looks like Heathcliff is taking us to Hollywood."

At the airport, the Nutmegs and Heathcliff get their tickets. "You'll have to put that cat in a cat carrier," says the lady at the ticket desk.

The nerve! thinks Heathcliff. He absolutely refuses to get into a cat carrier. A star should travel first class. Heathcliff won't go at all if he has to go in that cat carrier—and that's all there is to it!

Iggy Nutmeg sees a baby doll at the airport gift shop—and that gives him an idea. "I'd like to buy that doll," he tells the saleslady.

"How nice," says the lady. "Is it for your little sister?"

"No," answers Iggy. "It's for my cat."

LITTLE WONDER
CAT CARRIER

Iggy's plan works. He dresses Heathcliff up in the baby clothes that the doll wore.

"What a funny looking baby," whisper the flight attendants when they see Heathcliff. Heathcliff gives them a mean look.

Heathcliff is not very happy about being dressed up as a baby. *Stars don't dress like babies*, he thinks. But Heathcliff cheers up when he finds out that the airline is serving fish for dinner. Oh boy! Heathcliff's favorite.

"Oh! No!" yells the flight attendant. "That baby is eating all the fish dinners! Somebody stop him!"

The flight attendants are glad to see "baby" Heathcliff go when the plane finally lands in Hollywood.

The Nutmegs arrive at their hotel in Hollywood. They want to take naps because they are tired from their long trip. But not Heathcliff! He's not tired one bit. He wants to take a walk and see the sights.

"Don't get into trouble," warns Grandpa Nutmeg as he lets Heathcliff out of the room.

Heathcliff strolls toward the fancy houses of the stars. He daydreams about the fancy house he will have when he is a star. It will be filled with all his friends. There will be fresh fish and sweet cream served at each meal.

TOME
STAR!
HEAP
BIG!

Heathcliff hops a fence and finds himself in the middle of a backyard party. *They must have known I was coming*, thinks Heathcliff. *How thoughtful of them to have a party for me*.

Heathcliff helps himself to the shrimp. "Get out of here, you pesky cat," yells the maid.

Hmmmph, thinks Heathcliff. *She must not realize that I am the guest of honor.*

Heathcliff decides to give the guests a treat. He gets up and sings with the band. "Get out of here," cries the bandleader, throwing a book of music at Heathcliff.

Well, Heathcliff thinks. *He certainly doesn't know great singing when he hears it*.

Heathcliff sees something that makes him perk up. In the middle of the yard is a big goldfish pond. *Here I come*, thinks Heathcliff, running straight for the pond.

"Get that cat out of here!" yells everyone at once.

Heathcliff decides that this party is boring, anyway. He hops over the fence and continues his tour of Hollywood.

Heathcliff stops to look at the footprints of famous people that are pressed in cement at Grauman's Chinese Theatre. He can't wait to put his prints into cement once he's a famous TV star. Heathcliff sees some men preparing fresh cement for a new set of prints. *Why wait?* thinks Heathcliff. *I might as well give them my paw prints right now.*

Plop!!! Heathcliff pounces into the wet cement. He leaves four perfect paw prints. Too bad the men who poured the cement aren't as pleased as Heathcliff is.

"Scat you rotten cat!" they yell.

Gee, and I didn't even get the chance to sign my name, thinks Heathcliff.

Best

Heathcliff returns to his hotel. "Where have you been Heathcliff?" scolds Iggy. "It's almost time for you to film your Little Whiskers Cat Crunchies commercial."

I was visiting my fans, Heathcliff thinks.

The Nutmegs get in a cab and ride over to the TV studio. The commercial director welcomes them. "And this must be little Heathcliff," he says trying to pet Heathcliff.

Keep your hands off me. I'm the star of this show, thinks Heathcliff. He looks around the set. *Where's the makeup artist? Where's my chair? Where's my dressing room?* Heathcliff wonders.

"Okay, let's get started," says the director. "I want to start with an opening shot of Heathcliff enjoying his favorite cat food—Little Whiskers."

He tells Heathcliff to stand in front of the camera and eat his cat food, but when the director says,"Lights. Camera. Action." no one can find Heathcliff.

He'd rather share a tuna sandwich with the director's assistant than eat that Little Whiskers stuff any day!

ATTEN,
BUTTON,
BLISTER,
GLISTEN,
+
SMITH

"Let's try again," mutters the director angrily. "Put that cat in front of the food and keep him there."

The director gets the shot all set up again. "Okay. Take two," he calls. But once again, no Heathcliff.

Suddenly there is a terrible racket on the next set. Oh! No! Heathcliff is in the middle of a bird food commercial! And he thinks the birds are the food!

Sqwuak! Sqwuak! The birds are flying all over the place.

"Achoooooo!" sneezes the director when a feather lands on his nose.

"My birds! My birds!" yells the lady from the pet store who brought the birds.

"Get that cat out of here!" screams the director.

"I'll give you anything—anything—just take your cat home. Please!" begs the director. Heathcliff settles for a basket of shrimp, and he returns to the hotel with the Nutmegs.

"Oh, well," sigh the Nutmegs. "That's our Heathcliff. He'll always be a star to us."

The End